Lucy Taylor

The Story of Sir Henry Havelock

The Hero of Lucknow

Lucy Taylor

The Story of Sir Henry Havelock
The Hero of Lucknow

ISBN/EAN: 9783743395428

Manufactured in Europe, USA, Canada, Australia, Japa

Cover: Foto ©Raphael Reischuk / pixelio.de

Manufactured and distributed by brebook publishing software
(www.brebook.com)

Lucy Taylor

The Story of Sir Henry Havelock

The Story of
SIR HENRY HAVELOCK

The Hero of Lucknow

BY

LUCY TAYLOR

Author of "The Children's Champion, and the Victories he Won,"
"Going on Pilgrimage," "Fritz of Prussia,"
&c.   &c.

" The path of duty is the way to glory."

T. NELSON AND SONS
London, Edinburgh, and New York

1895

CONTENTS.

HAVELOCK.

CHAPTER I.

WHAT SHALL I BE?

" I 'VE nearly got it! Here goes for the next bough!
Hurrah, I'll have it now in a twinkling!"

But, alas! "there's many a slip between" the boy's
hand and the bird's nest. Snap! Crash went the
rotten branch; leaves, and twigs, and bits of broken
wood went flying down helter-skelter through the
green boughs beneath, a small boy very much mixed
up in the middle of them; while some birds flew out
with a shrill screech, laughing, perhaps, at the sorry
plight of the bold little plunderer. *Plump* came
something down on the turf, and then the something
picked itself up and rubbed its elbows, and, perhaps,
glanced a little ruefully at the ragged rent in its
jacket; but it didn't howl, or even seem much fright-
ened, and would, no doubt, have "swarmed" up the
tree again immediately, had not the unlucky branch
that offered the only chance of reaching the coveted
nest broken short off close to the trunk.

The "something" inside that jacket was going to

be a great general some day, but at present was only a very plucky little schoolboy of the stuff of which great men are made.

The boy's name was Henry Havelock, and he came of a brave fighting family, being descended from the bold Danish *Havelok* who ruled a part of our eastern coast long before the first Saxon king began to reign. But Henry's father never handled a sword. He con-tented himself with the more peaceful occupation of building ships; and it was at the seaport of Sunder-land that Henry was born, on the 5th of April 1795.

Henry's father made a great deal of money at ship-building, and bought a pretty park in Kent for his home; so, in the very first year of this nineteenth century, we find the boy riding to school in Dartford on his pony by the side of his elder brother. Those were not the days of "Kindergartens," so the little boy of five had to share the studies and the rough play of bigger lads, yes, and the rough usage, too; but, as he grew older, his brave spirit loved to defend the weak, even if he had to suffer for it.

One day Henry came into class with a black eye. "Havelock, what's the matter?" asked the master, who, though not over tender toward his pupils, dis-approved of reckless fighting. But Henry made no reply. "Tell me how you got that black eye," re-peated the master, the boys watching with great interest. "Who gave it you, and what have you been quarrelling about?"

"If you please, sir, I cannot tell you," was the quiet reply.

"But I insist on knowing," went on the master, looking annoyed.

Henry, however, refused to tell, and got a caning for his disobedience. The fact was he had interfered to prevent a younger boy being very cruelly used by one of the cowardly bullies of the school. The child could not defend himself, and brave Henry stood between him and his tormentor, fought the great hulking scoundrel, and got a black eye for his pains; but his idea of honour forbade him to "tell tales" of the big fellow who had given him the blow.

When ten years old, Henry Havelock went up to the Charterhouse, a big school in London, where he stayed till he was seventeen. Here he certainly found life no easier. Work was hard, punishments were severe and frequent, rules were stern and unbending, and all the younger boys were "fags." But Henry never complained, nor even seemed to think his lot at all a hard one; for he had no idea of idling away his schooldays, nor of shirking his duty. Play was all very well, and nobody enjoyed a game better than he, but there was no getting Havelock "up to larks" while work remained undone. "Old Phlos," as his companions called him (short for "Philosopher"), would grind steadily away at his books when the others were off to some uproarious game, and nothing would tempt him away till his task was finished. Sometimes, too, had you peeped quietly into one of the bedrooms, you would have seen a little group of boys on their knees. Henry had not forgotten those happy half-hours at home, when mother had read and prayed with him and his three brothers; and now he had persuaded four companions to hold a little prayer-meeting by themselves. When he was nearly fifteen, that good mother died rather suddenly, and Henry was so shocked and broken-hearted that it was a long time before he could at all forget his loss.

Those early days of the century were eventful ones for Europe, and Henry Havelock read the daily papers eagerly. Wellington was fighting the French in Spain; for Napoleon threatened the safety of our island home, after having humiliated Prussia, and marched his conquering armies over half the Continent. Nelson had fallen at the moment of victory at Trafalgar, when young Havelock was but ten years old, and Napoleon triumphed but a few months later at Austerlitz; while, in 1809, Sir John Moore was laid in his soldier's grave by the ramparts of Corunna in the gray dawn of a January morning.

Until his disastrous retreat from Moscow, it seemed that the Emperor of France was to be master in Europe; and though afterwards defeated at Leipzig, and retiring to Elba, it was not till the great day of Waterloo that the power of the dreaded tyrant was finally broken. When the welcome news of that glorious and hard-won victory rang joyously through the length and breadth of England, setting bells pealing and bonfires blazing, Henry Havelock was just twenty years of age.

By this time the pleasant home in Kent had, alas! been sold, Mr. Havelock having lost so much money that he could no longer live there, and the family had removed to Clifton.

"What shall I be?" young Henry had naturally asked himself on leaving school, and as his mother had wished him to study law, and had prophesied that her boy would some day "sit on the woolsack," he made up his mind to the dry reading and the big law books, and began his studies in 1813. But Henry Havelock never got far toward the "woolsack." He was to handle the sword, not the pen; to wear the trim red coat, not the flowing wig and gown. His father, displeased about something, refused to pay his expenses any longer, and, therefore, as a lawyer's training costs a great deal, the young student had to give it up.

But the future path was soon made plain. Henry's elder brother was already a soldier, and came back with glowing stories of brave deeds on the field of Waterloo. Henry soon caught up William's martial spirit, and before long he too was a soldier. And now his books are all changed. No more tedious State trials to pore over, nor wordy Acts of Parliament, but thrilling stories of conflict and struggle, of valour and victory. Not that it was, by any means, all fun learning to be a soldier; for tactics and military routine, and the details of company, and regiment, and battalion, and division, are dry enough reading: there is nothing, indeed, that is worth learning that can be mastered without *real hard work* and plenty of "grit." To endure, to obey, and to *keep at it*, are the first duties of a soldier.

And it was the schoolboy who never shirked his lessons, who never thought it a fine thing to go larking with duties undone and then tell lies about it, who dared to do right in the teeth of a roar of senseless laughter,—it was he who now took up his new studies with all his might, and showed the world that he had the making in him of the dauntless British soldier; indeed, it was afterwards said that few English officers ever understood their profession more thoroughly than he.

But Waterloos are not fought every day, and young Havelock found soldiering rather dull work.   It is quite possible, to be sure, to be a hero in times of peace ; but not the sort of hero of whom the world takes much notice, and humdrum, obscure duties are apt to grow rather wearisome.   For nearly eight years Henry Havelock served in the army at home ; but there was no " Bony " now to fear or to fight, and the " Battle of Glasgow Green," as the young soldier called it, when his regiment was called out to help in putting down rioters, was his only experience of firing in real earnest.

Henry's two brothers, William and Charles, both soldiers, went out to India in 1821 and 1822 ; and Henry, hopeless of seeing any fighting in peaceful England, followed them a year later, as a lieutenant in the 13th Light Infantry, going to Calcutta, and fitting himself for his new post by a diligent study of Hindustani.   The voyage was an eventful one. His mother's prayers, and the little prayer-meetings at school which had often cost him dear, could, surely, never have been utterly forgotten ; but barrack life had, alas ! put almost everything but soldiering out of mind.   God had been set aside, and fame and glory became the chief objects of desire.   But the words of a humble fellow-soldier changed, while out on the broad ocean, the whole current of his thoughts. James Gardner induced his companion, Henry Havelock, to read the Bible with him, and pointed out to him the great gift of God to the world in his only Son, and the great sacrifice once offered for sinners. Havelock read, thought, and prayed.   The light of the knowledge of the glory of God in the face of

Jesus Christ broke in on his soul; he sought forgiveness at the feet of his Saviour, and took that Saviour henceforth as his Captain and his King. Havelock landed in India a Christian; fearless, outspoken, and thorough-going in his religion, as in everything else, and feeling that now he had always a divine Friend at his side, so that, indeed, he need "fear no evil."

But being a Christian did not mean being a milksop; neither did Havelock imagine for a moment that God was going to make life all smooth and easy without his troubling about the matter. Rather did his love for Christ make him more industrious and earnest than ever, eager also to help others as well as to improve himself.

It was May when the *General Kyd* reached Calcutta, for she had been all round by the Cape, and such a voyage took much longer in those days than it does now. The barracks at Fort William, near the town, were most uncomfortably crowded, and as the officers could not have even a small room to themselves, Havelock chose James Gardner as his companion. Here he stayed nearly a year, meeting the good Bishop Heber and other missionaries, teaching the men under his command, and setting such a bright example in the discharge of his duties, that although some might sneer at the "Methodist," nobody could afford to despise the soldier.

CHAPTER II.

"HAVELOCK'S SAINTS."

HAVELOCK had not to wait very long in India before there came a call to active service. In 1824 war broke out in Burmah, and Havelock's regiment was ordered off to Rangoon to defend British possessions.

As the rest of our story will all be about India and places near, it will be well to see just how these countries lie, and to whom they belong. Almost in the middle of the map of Asia lies the great tongue of India, a country much bigger than the British Isles, even with the Irish Sea included. When Havelock landed in Calcutta, the English had been masters in India for about sixty-six years. Three large tracts of country were ruled by British Governors: the Bengal Presidency, the Madras Presidency, and the Bombay Presidency. Madras and Bombay you will easily find on the east and west coasts. The capital of the Bengal Presidency is Calcutta, which, with its defence of Fort William, lies close to the mouth of the Ganges, on the north-east of India. The rest of the land is under native princes, and the whole is under the direction of a Governor-General appointed by the British Government.

Now such a large country as India, of course, wants a good deal of protection, and we have to watch pretty narrowly what our neighbours on either side are doing. On the west lies Afghanistan, where many a brave British soldier has found a grave; for we have to take care that nobody gets in through those great mountain passes to disturb the peace of India. We are afraid of Persia trying to secure Herat, and then letting in the Russian bear, which would never do. Herat is much too near India for it to be safe to allow a great Power to get hold of it.

On the east lies another big tongue of country made up of Burmah, Siam, and Cochin China. Part of Burmah—a little strip running down the west side—belonged to us, and it was here that Havelock fought his first battle. The rest of Burmah was ruled by a native monarch, and the king was beginning to interfere with our provinces, so, in April 1824, an army of 10,000 men under Sir Archibald Campbell was sent to defend British Burmah.

But Havelock did not see the first of the fighting. While Rangoon was being taken he was waiting impatiently for the wind to fill the sails and take him across the Bay of Bengal. It came at last, to be sure, and he and his troops landed safely; but no true soldier likes to miss an important battle.

Burmah is a land of mighty temples and gross idolatry. After the victory, the gigantic idol in the great Rangoon temple held the colours of the British regiments in its outstretched arms, and the Temple of Gaudama was devoted to the worship of Jehovah. But there was no minister to read and pray with those soldiers who cared to leave the noisy revelry of the victorious camp for the service of God, so Havelock gathered his men about him in a side chapel of the gay pagoda, and held a little service. It was a curious sight. Cross-legged images of Buddha, the favourite Burmese god, were arranged all round the room, and in the lap of every one of them was an oil lamp. In the middle stood Havelock, surrounded by the soldiers of his regiment, singing God's praises in the very faces of the senseless idols.

But although Rangoon was taken, the war was not ended. The enemy stood ready to fight just outside the town, protected by *stockades* (enclosures fenced round with big, pointed sticks) which were not at all easy to force. Havelock took one of these stockades, a task which he found the native Madras soldiers could not manage without the help of some Englishmen. Fever, however, proved a harder foe to fight, and our brave soldier was soon taken ill and sent back to Calcutta, and even ordered to return to England. But Havelock was very unwilling to take so long a voyage, and only went as far as Bombay, where he was received by Elphinstone, the Governor of the Bombay Presidency. In rather less than a year he was so much better that he went back to Burmah, welcomed gladly by his men, with whom he at once began again their meetings for reading and prayer. Of course such doings were jeered at unmercifully, but he who had stood his ground at school showed no signs now of flinching in the camp. The men, too, got their share of ridicule, being nicknamed "Havelock's saints."

But those who laughed at them in barracks did not dare to despise them in battle. One day a sudden attack was made by the enemy when most of the soldiers were quite unfit for action. Thinking all was safe, they had been drinking heavily. "Call out Havelock's saints," rang out the general's shrill order through the camp. "*They* are never drunk when wanted, and Havelock himself is always ready!" Instantly the sober, God-fearing men, prompt and ready, sprang to arms, shouldered their muskets, and, with a ringing cheer, followed their beloved leader, bravely facing the foe, and very soon driving them back in utter rout and confusion.

Soon after this Havelock joined the Baptists at Serampore, and married Harriet Marshman, the daughter of one of the missionaries. While lying ill a report was brought to him that one of the men in his regiment was drunk. Of course he was very grieved, and made inquiry as soon as possible, but was delighted to find that the culprit was *not* one of his men, after all, though his name happened to be exactly the same. Well might Colonel Sale exclaim, "I know nothing about Baptists; but I only wish *all* the men in the army were Baptists, for 'Havelock's saints' never have a black mark against their names, nor are they ever found in the lock-up." That is the kind of thing that real out-and-out Christianity does for the British soldier.

The Burmese War ended with the king signing a treaty of peace, giving up the country he had stolen, and paying something toward the expenses of the war. There was a grand ceremony at Ava to receive the treaty, and Havelock was sent, with other British officers, to meet the king. Eastern monarchs like to do everything with great show and magnificence, and the scene at the king's court was a very gay one. Jewels, and gilding, and gorgeous robes were abundantly displayed, for no end of homage must be paid to "The Lord of the White Elephant." Splendid presents were given and received; the treaty was signed; Havelock and his companions were made Burmese nobles with very high-sounding titles, which they were not at all likely to make use of; then the British army was withdrawn from Burmah, and Havelock found himself once more on the shores of India.

For some time there was no more fighting to do. Havelock was moved about a good deal during the next twelve years, fulfilling various duties at different stations of the British army. Calcutta, Serampore, Dinapore, Cawnpore, Gwalior, and Agra were the chief places he visited; all of which lie near to the river Ganges, on which Havelock travelled to and fro very often. During these years his three sons were born. The eldest was named "Henry." "Lionel" was proposed for the name of the second son, but Havelock objected. "No," said he; "we have enough *lions* in our family. I want the rest to be *lambs*." So the boy was called "Joshua," and never entered the army; but Henry made as brave a *lion* as his father. The third little son died; indeed it was wonderful that any of them lived, for few English children can bear the burning heat of India. The want of a doctor's help was also felt then much more than it is now. One of Havelock's little ones suffered terribly in cutting its teeth; and as they were on the river at the time, there was no one at hand to lance the little feverish gums and relieve the pain. But baby's father was not the man to stand by and say "I can't," and let the poor little sufferer die in convulsions. With a trembling hand and a very tender heart he took out his penknife, and made way through the swollen gums for the tooth to come, and was rewarded by seeing his boy lose all the pain and burning fever, and drop off into a refreshing sleep. In a few days little Henry was quite well, and lived to grow up a valiant soldier and win the Victoria Cross.

A great part of Havelock's time was taken up now in drilling and training his men, and also in teaching them, holding prayer-meetings and services, and preaching to them. He was very earnest, too, in doing battle against the soldier's deadly enemy, *strong drink*. In those days temperance work was laughed at as quite nonsensical, and abstainers were looked upon as little less than lunatics; for people had not then learned how very *much* harm even a *little* drink can do, nor how well the hardest work under a burning sun, or among polar snows, may be done without any of it—indeed how much safer are both the Indian soldier and the Arctic sailor without "grog." But if Havelock did not then know all that we do to-day, he could not take the command of a regiment without seeing what a dreadful temptation drink was to his men. Though he was never an abstainer, he succeeded, for the most part, in keeping his men steady and sober; and while at Agra, he formed a Temperance Society among them and got a coffee-room built. Chapels, too, were provided near to the barracks, and while on the march Havelock gathered the men together for worship in the open air. But although he won the love and devotion of all his soldiers, no man under Havelock's command might hope to neglect his duty and escape punishment. *Instant* obedience, without a question or a murmur, he demanded from every man; but then he was *himself* prepared to render the same obedience to those above him in command. His keen, watchful eye quickly found out a culprit, and stern sentence promptly followed a fault; yet he was careful to control his own somewhat fiery temper, and to show his men that he trusted them, and expected them to behave like true Britons, both in the barracks and in the field. And it was the Christian men who always fought the best. "Those," said Havelock, "who fear God will fear man least, and the right hands that know their way between the leaves of well-worn Bibles, always wield the sword most bravely and brilliantly."

During this time of peace Havelock studied languages a good deal, perfecting himself in Hindustani and learning Persian, so that he was able to act as interpreter for those who did not understand these Eastern tongues. Just before war broke out afresh, he was promoted to a higher rank in the army, and when 15,000 men were sent across the Indus into Afghanistan, *Captain* Havelock marched at the head of his column.

CHAPTER III.

MARCHING WESTWARD.

YOU will remember that when looking at the map of Asia to see how India lies, with Burmah on the east and Afghanistan on the west, you found the town of Herat, which, though so near to Persia, we are very careful that neither Persia nor Russia shall get hold of. Though *British* possessions in Asia are the most important, *Russian* possessions there are much larger; and England and Russia are always watching that great continent, and trying to grab more little bits for themselves. England fancies that Russia would be very glad to get India for itself, so the British lion, like a dog with a bone, begins to growl when he thinks Russia is coming at all too near.

Now, in 1833, Persia had tried to take Herat, and in 1837 she was busy collecting an army again; so we sent Captain Burnes to Cabul, the capital of Afghanistan, to watch what was being done. Dost Mahomet was then ruler or "Ameer" of Afghanistan, and he was very anxious to get help from England, because old Runjeet Singh, one of the Indian princes, had taken a bit of his country away from him. But England would not listen to anything he had to say, and the Russian bear, watching his chance, stepped up and said he would be most happy to help; so the Czar and the Ameer became good friends, and joined together against British power.

When England heard of it she was very angry, and made up her mind to dethrone Dost Mahomet, and to put in his place a contemptible old Ameer whom the Afghans had turned out. His name was Shah Soojah, and he lived, at our expense, at Loodiana in the Punjâb, where the wicked, drunken old Runjeet Singh was prince. Meanwhile the Shah of Persia marched his army up to Herat and besieged it, frightening the natives of India so much that, even in the Deccan, a province more than a thousand miles away, men buried their money and jewels, to hide them from the conquering army which, they imagined, was going to march through the land.

Herat, however, never needed the presence of a British army. After trying for ten months to take the city, the Shah, alarmed at the warlike preparations of the British, gave up the attempt and went home. But England was determined to have her way about Shah Soojah, so the British army marched through the rocky passes on the west of the Punjâb, crossed burning plains and dreary wildernesses, and at last, after a four months' journey by a most roundabout road, reached Candahar, a city lying a good deal farther south-west than Cabul. But the troops bringing the new Ameer found no enemy ready for them when they marched up to the gates. This was fortunate, for they were worn out and half-starved. It was now April, and the harvest could not be gathered till June; so, as it was impossible to go forward to Cabul without corn, the army stopped at Candahar for two months. By the end of July, after a three weeks' march, the soldiers came in sight of the strong fortress of Ghuznee, of which the Afghans were very proud, and which was now filled with soldiers led by Akbar Khan, the son of Dost Mahomet. Captain Havelock, who was riding forward with the commander of the Bengal division, Sir Willoughby Cotton, was one of the first to catch sight of the gray fort peeping through the trees, and he feared that even the bravest soldiers would never be able to take it without the help of the very big cannon which had been left behind at Candahar.

But Sir John Keane, who led the Bombay division of the army, had another plan. He drew off the attention of the Afghans by attacking them on the south of the fort, while two bold men crept across the bridge in the darkness of night, and piled up at the gate 900 lbs. of gunpowder. This was fired; the gate was blown to pieces; and, at the sound of the bugle, a storming party, which had been placed close by, rushed in among the smoking ruins, beating down the sharp swords of the furious Afghans. It was a hard struggle, but the enemy gave way at last, five hundred of them being found dead within the fort. The British flag waved on the walls, and a quantity of food, horses, and weapons was secured by the conquerors. Fortunately there was no strong drink among the spoil, for Afghans are followers of Mohammed, who forbids them to take intoxicating drink. Havelock tells us how much more merciful and generous to their foes were the victorious English soldiers, simply because they were quite sober; for when excited by spirits, soldiers will do many wicked and cruel things that they would otherwise scorn as vile and detestable.

After this it was easy to go forward to Cabul; at least there was no more fighting to do, for Dost Mahomet had run away. So, on the 7th of August, Havelock joined in a very gay procession, in which Shah Soojah was taken through the streets of the capital and established in the palace. But it was very plain that, although his subjects dared not resist a British army, they did not at all relish the new Ameer, nor mean to obey him. What, then, was to be done? The war was over; but if the army returned home, Shah Soojah would be knocked over like a senseless dummy directly the last redcoat was out of sight, and all the work would be undone in a day. So there was nothing for it but to leave some of the soldiers who put him on the throne, to hold him there.   Sir Willoughby Cotton took the command of this " Army of Occupation."

But Havelock went back to Serampore, for he was anxious to write a book about the war, hoping it would bring him money to help to pay for his boys' education.   Unhappily " The War in Afghanistan " never did this, though Havelock knew nothing of the disappointment when he started to return to Cabul with General Elphinstone, who was to take the place of Sir Willoughby Cotton.   Poor General Elphinstone was quite unfit for his duties, for he had gout so very badly that sometimes he could hardly move about, and when in severe pain he could not think, or plan, or direct those under him.   When the travellers reached Cabul they found things in a very bad state. The palace, instead of being well defended by soldiers, was filled with Shah Soojah's wives and children and servants ; the British troops were stationed some distance out of the city ; while the natives were not at all inclined to be submissive and peaceful.   Still, Macnaughten, the envoy (who was sent to Cabul as a sort of governor), thought all was safe.

But, unfortunately, the British Government had made a terrible blunder.   The mountain passes between India and Afghanistan were full of robbers, who attacked every one they could lay hands on They were so fierce, and there were so many of them, that they did pretty much as they pleased, and the British, therefore, offered them £8,000 a year for peace and quietness.   The money had been paid, and the chiefs had kept their promises ; nobody was hurt and nothing stolen.   But just now the English thought they need not pay so much, and cut down the £8,000 to £4,000. The chiefs were enraged, murdered and robbed again as before, blocking up the road, and making it impossible for any traveller to pass from the one country to the other in safety.

When Havelock reached Cabul he was quite alarmed at the state of things. Here, on the outskirts of a town which had scarcely any defence, was placed a small British army, separated from its own territory by hundreds of miles, the space between being filled with savage enemies. Dost Mahomet, to be sure, had been taken prisoner, but his son, Akbar Khan, eager for revenge, had collected a large army, and was watching his opportunity to fall on the hated English. Macnaughten and Elphinstone were both anxious to leave; the former to be appointed Governor of Bombay, and the latter because he was so worn out with pain that he was quite unable to do his duty. But they could not at present get away in safety, and Havelock, therefore, went out under General Sale to fight the fierce foes and to clear the road.

This expedition was the means of saving Havelock's life, though at the time he left Cabul the place of safety seemed to be with General Elphinstone in the city, and the place of danger with General Sale. On that autumn morning in 1841, when Havelock marched out of the capital, he had been reading the 39th chapter of Jeremiah, and the words spoken to Ebedmelech seemed almost like a prophecy: "Thus saith the Lord of hosts, the God of Israel; Behold, I will bring my words upon this city for evil, and not for good; and they shall be accomplished in that day before thee. But I will deliver thee in that day, saith the Lord : and thou shalt not be given into the hand of the men of whom thou art afraid. For I will surely deliver thee, and thou shalt not fall by the sword, but thy life shall be for a prey unto thee : because thou hast put thy trust in me, saith the Lord."

Very soon Havelock found himself in the midst of hard fighting ; for the Afghans, armed to the teeth, thronged the narrow defiles and fired down from the lofty precipices, fighting like wild cats when the British encountered them in hand-to-hand conflict. But by the 3rd of October the British force succeeded in reaching a town called Gundamuck, and Sale was sent for by Elphinstone to return with all the troops to Cabul, if he could safely leave the sick and wounded. But this was impossible ; neither could Sale, who was badly wounded, spare Havelock from his side. After eighteen days' rest, therefore, they pressed on, fighting their way to Jelalabad, another city on the Cabul River, lying in the midst of fruitful orchards, and containing the winter palace of the Ameer. Havelock, and his friend Captain George Broadfoot, had advised that all weapons should be taken from the native troops left in Gundamuck ; but this was not thought needful, and directly the British troops were out of sight, they rebelled, and blew up the powder magazine their officers escaping with great difficulty.

Meanwhile things were getting worse and worse at Cabul. There had been a riot in the town, when two English officers were murdered ; and yet a few hundreds out of the five thousand British troops close by could easily have restored order. But everything seemed going wrong. Elphinstone and Macnaughten could not agree, and all was confusion and dismay. Very soon after, Macnaughten was killed and poor Elphinstone was taken prisoner.

But General Sale, not knowing the worst, prepared to defend himself in Jelalabad against the Afghans swarming all round the walls. It was very difficult work, and, indeed, seemed almost impossible; for the defences of the town were so broken down and ruinous that Havelock and his companions, like Nehemiah at Jerusalem, could hardly get round the walls to see their condition; and meanwhile fierce troops of Afghans came dashing up to make sudden attacks, and had to be driven back over and over again. Had it not been for Captain Broadfoot, there would have been hardly a hope of defending the town; but while in Cabul, this officer had insisted on being supplied with proper tools for his sappers and miners, whose work was no less important than that of the soldiers, though they did no fighting. Broadfoot's superiors had not thought his demand of much consequence, and but for his own undaunted spirit he would have come away without the tools, and no guns or swords could ever have done the work of spades and pick-axes. But Broadfoot had carried out his purpose. He had hunted up smiths and set them to make the tools he wanted, whether they liked it or not, with soldiers standing over them till it was done. And now, in the hour of need, he was well supplied; and the strong arms of the sturdy workmen began at once to dig ditches, and build walls and ramparts on which to place the cannon. Broadfoot found, too, that the work—and it was *very* hard work—was done better on short food allowance and *no* grog, than it would had the men been able to have sufficient food, and, together with it, the coveted dram. Heads were clear and hands were strong, and in a few weeks all was ready to beat off the foe. And the work was not done a minute too soon, for thousands of bloodthirsty Afghans were now coming round the town and beginning to fire heavily on the little band of British. Powder and shot were running rather low, and as little as possible must be used; but the enemy were driven back so successfully that, for a time, Jelalabad and its garrison were left in peace.

CHAPTER IV.

A GALLANT DEFENCE.

BAD news now came in from Cabul. " We are in great peril," wrote Elphinstone; "cannot you come and help us?" Very soon followed the news of the envoy's murder, and an order from Elphinstone to Sale to return to India. But this order had been signed when the poor general was entirely in the enemy's hands, and General Sale refused to obey it, although Akbar Khan was triumphing over the " Feringhees," as he called the English, and gathering all his Afghans to surround Jelalabad, and prevent the inhabitants from getting any food. Some officers thought it would be well to abandon the city; but Sale, Broadfoot, and Havelock stood firm, like true Britons. " We will *never* retreat before the foe," said they, " without orders from home to do so. We will hold the town till the last; and if we cannot be victorious, we can at least die with swords in our hands." It was hoped, too, that help was near; but the troops sent out under Colonel Wyld were hindered so much on the way that, at last, it was found impossible to advance at all, and a message was sent on to General Sale to say that Jelalabad must take care of itself.

This was not very encouraging, especially as news was coming in of the dreadful condition of the British who had left Cabul and started for Jelalabad. It was mid-winter, and the arrival of the forlorn travellers was anxiously expected. But, alas! only *one* solitary Englishman ever reached Jelalabad in safety. On the 13th of January some officers watching from the flat roof of a high house for any sign of the band of wayfarers, caught sight of a single figure in the distance. Field-glasses were eagerly raised, and it was soon seen that the traveller wore English dress, and rode a little hill-pony, so jaded and exhausted it could hardly put one foot before another. A signal was made which the horseman understood, for he waved a soldier's cap over his head and pressed eagerly forward. The officers rushed to the gate and threw it open to welcome their countryman, who almost fell from his pony into their arms, for he was half-starved, terribly bruised and cut, and so overcome with the horror of that awful journey that he could scarcely speak till he had taken rest and food. But the few words he hurriedly stammered out fell like ice on the warm hearts of the brave defenders of Jelalabad. The stranger proved to be Dr. Brydon, an army doctor, and he told them that a company of nearly 15,000 people, a great number of them English, trusting that, as they had given up Cabul, their foes would allow them to retreat unhurt, had started for Jelalabad; but they had no sooner entered the dreadful mountain passes, now blocked with snow, than they were surrounded and attacked.

General Sale, therefore, concluded that a crowd of hunted fugitives might be expected to hurry toward the city, followed by their cruel and treacherous foes; perhaps even now, indeed, they were being murdered quite close at hand. Horsemen were sent out to meet and protect them, for there was not an English soldier in the town who would not freely encounter any danger in the hope of saving his comrades. The cavalry galloped out for two miles, while a huge bonfire flared on the walls to guide the steps of the wanderers. But there was no sign of a single fugitive, and the horsemen returned, weary and disappointed, and with a horrible dread weighing on their hearts. Through the night the light still blazed high, and every half-hour the bugler sounded the stirring call to "advance," to encourage the way-worn travellers and proclaim a welcome. Another day passed, and still the strongest spy-glass failed to reveal one solitary figure. For three nights sounded the cheery bugle-note; but, alas! there was no reply to its summons, for, clear and shrill as it sounded through the valley, it could not bid the *dead* awake! Fainting in weariness, benumbed with cold by night, scorched by the sun by day, exhausted with hunger, shot down by muskets levelled from the precipices, surprised by hidden bands of heartless murderers, the vast multitude dropped, one by one, or fell in heaps of slain on the reddened snow-drift or the rocky ledge, many a mile being thickly strown with their slaughtered bodies; for the Mohammedan thinks it a glory to stain his sword with the blood of the "Infidel," or even to die fighting the "Feringhee."

A weary sadness fell on the hearts of the defenders of Jelalabad when the last hopes died out. The Sunday after Dr. Brydon's arrival Havelock assembled his men in the open square, and read the church service and the 46th Psalm. Sorely did the sturdy little company need to be reminded that "God is our refuge and strength:" they were in dreadful distress, cut off from their friends, exposed all around to merciless enemies, and with famine and disease close upon them. And there seemed no chance of any help By the end of the month an impudent letter came in from Shah Soojah, saying a treaty had been signed, and the English had agreed to leave the country. Added to this, the Government in India made little effort to send aid, and did not seem to understand that to allow the Afghans to triumph would endanger the safety of all our possessions in India. General Sale now began to waver and to talk of making terms with Akbar Khan; but Havelock and his friend Broadfoot would not hear of giving in, or of listening to the lying promises of a deceitful foe.

Could we have peeped into the general's head-quarters in Jelalabad one January morning in 1842, we should have seen a little gathering of officers very eagerly talking over the condition of affairs, and deciding what was to be done. Though it is the middle of winter, they are sitting out of doors, shaded from the hot sunshine by a trellis covered with creepers, while a cool fountain sends up its sparkling water in the middle of the enclosed court. We talk about a "changeable climate" in England, but in Afghanistan it is far more changeable—only there it is easy to say *what* the change will be, and here it is quite impossible. In winter there is a hard frost at night, and by day it is hotter than we ever have it in England; indeed it once actually happened that a soldier was *frozen* to death at night, and the next day, at noon, another was killed by *sunstroke*.

A long and keen discussion was held in that Eastern garden; but, happily, it was decided not to yield one inch to the foe, nor to think either of making a treaty with the enemy or of abandoning the city. Everybody seemed in better spirits when there was no more thought of surrender; and though there was so little food that nobody had enough to eat, all the men worked with hearty goodwill, and Havelock tells us that, in spite of great danger, all was " health, cheerfulness, industry, and resolution." Fortunately, there was no rum left, so there were much fewer men than usual in the hospital and lock-up, and work was done with a stronger arm and a sweeter temper. Even a great misfortune, which came upon the garrison in February, could not damp the men's energy and courage. Quite suddenly a terrible shock of earthquake utterly destroyed the defences prepared with so much labour, exposing the city once more to the attacks of the enemy just when Akbar Khan himself was making his appearance in the valley. But instead of giving way to despair, the men worked harder than ever, repaired the great rents made in the walls, built up the ruined earthworks, replaced the cannon in

position, and, in a month's time, everything was so
thoroughly restored to order, that Akbar Khan, on
coming in sight of the city, imagined that the English
had kept off the earthquake by witchcraft, and became,
accordingly, much more afraid of them ; so that what
seemed such a dreadful misfortune, turned out to be
a means of protection. Akbar Khan himself had
suffered terribly, for many of his followers had been
killed by the earthquake and many more had run
away in terror.

At last it was resolved to make an attack on
Akbar Khan. The rebel chief was now about two
miles away, at the head of six thousand men, while
General Sale had only about fourteen hundred to
march out against him, and these were not all British
soldiers. Captain Broadfoot had been very badly
wounded, and was unable to lead his division, so
Havelock took the command of about three hundred
and fifty men when the little army set out at sunrise
on the 7th of April.

And the brave captain had some very hard fighting
to do that day. Fifteen hundred mounted Afghans,
with wild cries and flashing sabres, galloped down
on his little band drawn up in a square to meet the
attack. Straight forward on to the levelled bayonets
rode their desperate chief, but his men hung back a
little as they came nearer. Dozens of them dropped
from their horses, stricken down by the shower of
bullets, and trampled to death in the wild charge, and
very soon the fierce fire from the muskets of that
sturdy little British company drove back the horsemen
in rout and confusion. Havelock himself narrowly
escaped the brandished swords of his infuriated foes.

In the hottest moment of the strife his horse threw him, and had not two soldiers of his own beloved 13th Regiment sprung forward to save their commander, the Afghans would have speedily made an end of the hated "Infidel." But long before the sun was high in the heavens, the battle was over, and the Afghans utterly swept away from their position; Akbar Khan had fled, his cannon were captured, and his camp burned.

Thus the British force, without any aid whatever, had finally delivered itself from its perilous position, and scattered its foes. Exactly the same thing ought to have been done at Cabul; but though the numbers there were greater, and the men not one whit less brave, their *commanders* were very different men, and did not know how to secure victory and safety. Poor Elphinstone could think of nothing but his torturing pain, and his chances of getting back to India; while under him was a colonel who, though very courageous, was "disqualified," we are told, "by infirmity of temper:" that is only a polite way of saying that he could not rule himself; therefore, of course, he could never hope to rule others.

But while the troops in Jelalabad were rejoicing over their "crowning mercy," as Havelock called it, help, not now so much needed, was close at hand. General Pollock had fought his way through the terrible Khyber Pass two days before the defeat of Akbar Khan, and reached the town a fortnight later. Of course the British were very glad to see their friends, though, perhaps, a little proud of having done so well without their help. As they marched joyfully into Jelalabad, with colours flying, the band welcomed them with merry music; the tune chosen, however, was the old Jacobite air, "Oh, but ye've been lang a-comin'!"

But there was stern work yet to be done. General Pollock marched on to Cabul, Sale and his troops following. On the road they met Akbar Khan, and a furious fight took place. The British soldiers were stirred to frenzy at the sight of the bodies of their murdered comrades strewed about on every hand, and even built up by the savage foe into their defences. Fresh dead fell thickly on the bones of Elphinstone's forces, so cruelly slaughtered in January during that fatal retreat; Akbar was finally defeated, and the victorious British took possession of his capital. Elphinstone had died while a prisoner but the rest of the captives were now set free, and gladly rejoined their countrymen in Cabul.

All faces were now turned homewards, and the troops, after marching safely through the once perilous Khyber Pass, crossed the Indus, and, on reaching the banks of the Sutlej in December, found Lord Ellenborough, the new Governor-General of India, waiting to receive the victorious army with all due honours.

The Afghan War, however, though it was full of the record of gallant deeds and noble endurance, had resulted in nothing at all except a fearful waste of gold and of precious life. We had come back conquerors at last, it is true, but we had utterly failed in our attempt to put Shah Soojah on the throne; and, so far from having increased the strength of our rule in India, our subjects there were gradually drifting into discontent and lawlessness, which, before another fifteen years had passed, would break out into open mutiny, threatening to drive us altogether from its shores, and to expose every British settlement in the land to a hideous massacre.

CHAPTER V.

FIGHTING SIKHS AND PERSIANS.

VERY welcome must have been those peaceful months which Havelock was now able to spend with his wife at Simla.   As the quiet holiday drew to a close, he was promoted to a higher rank in the army, and, in October 1843, was called to join the new Commander-in-Chief, Sir Hugh Gough, as his Persian interpreter.

The camp was at Cawnpore, a city which, together with Lucknow, will always be remembered in connection with the name of our hero.   Havelock reached Cawnpore just in time to join in fresh fighting; for a quarrel had broken out with the Mahrattas close by, and a war followed, very short, it is true, but costing a great many lives.

The British army did not, at first, know what a stubborn foe they were about to meet, and marched out to battle with the idea that the expedition would be a nice little picnic.   One of the generals, whose body was that night left on the field of death, boastfully declared that he should want no other weapon than a horsewhip; and so great was the feeling of security, that not only were the heavy cannon left behind, but a number of ladies, mounted on elephants, joined the march, as the guests of the Governor-General.

But everything did not go so smoothly as was expected. Suddenly, with a roar like thunder, a cannon-ball came crashing by and carried off one of the ears of a gaily-harnessed elephant; and it was only after a good deal of confusion that the troops were got into order to meet the enemy, who seemed by no means inclined to run away. Havelock was to be seen in the thickest of the fight, cool and calm, with the deadly bullets cutting up the ground all round him. He succeeded in leading to the charge a regiment of Indian soldiers who seemed to be in no hurry to get too near the enemy.

After this little campaign was over, Havelock enjoyed two more quiet years, travelling about with Sir Hugh Gough, and meeting his old friend Major Broadfoot once more, whom now, alas! he was so soon to lose on a fresh battle-field. The old rascal, Runjeet Singh, was dead; his son, too, died in 1840, in spite of medicine made of emerald dust. The Sikhs are the very best native soldiers in India, having been trained by European officers, and just now they were a good deal more than their own ruler, a native queen, knew how to manage. So her highness thought it would be a good plan to set them invading British territory, especially as they had got it into their heads that it would be easy now to conquer the Feringhee, and turn him out of the country. And it was not very strange that these Indians should have such a notion, for they had beaten the Afghans, which the English seemed to find a very difficult matter.

The struggle took place on the banks of the Sutlej River. The British army was taken by surprise at Moodkee, and only roused to action by Broadfoot's prompt warning. Havelock again led a reluctant regiment to the charge. The men, who were scarcely a match for the splendid Sikhs, were turning round and preparing to run before the foe, when Havelock galloped up, shouting that the enemy was "in front, not behind," when the soldiers returned to the charge for very shame. General Sale, whom we remember at Jelalabad, fell in this battle, and Havelock, though he escaped without even a wound, had two horses killed under him.

But a much more important battle was that of Ferozeshah, in which, unhappily, the good Major Broadfoot lost his life. When night closed in it was impossible to claim victory for British arms, and the Sikhs were murdering the wounded in the bitter cold of the open field; but, happily for us, our enemies quarrelled among themselves and robbed their general, who fled. At daybreak, then, they were easily scattered, and two days after every Sikh soldier had disappeared. But we paid dear for the victory, for nearly seven hundred men were killed; and the work was not yet done, for the Sikhs were gallant fighters and soon returned to the charge. A tremendous battle was fought at Sobraon, in which the British were repulsed over and over again, losing more than two thousand men. But the Sikhs lost *eight* thousand, and were at last driven over the Sutlej, where hundreds were drowned in the deep river, the current being quite choked with dead bodies.

With that the war ended, and Havelock escaped

quite unhurt, though, when another horse fell under him at Sobraon, the ball passed within an inch of his body. Grieving sorely for the loss of his friend Major Broadfoot, he kept his beautiful Arab for his own use, and had two bullets taken out of the poor animal, which quite recovered from its wounds. Havelock had learned a great deal of the art of war by this time; but feeling how much *more* there was yet to learn, he modestly writes: "I entered on this war thinking myself something of a soldier. I have now found out that I know nothing; but, happily, I am not too old to learn."

But there were no more lessons to learn, just yet, on the battle-field; for although, in 1848, a Second Sikh War broke out, Havelock took no share in it. He had been travelling with the Governor-General in the Punjâb, visiting Lahore, and seeing some of the famous Sikh chiefs—cunning, hypocritical fellows; but after his return to Bombay, he was taken ill with fever, brought on, very likely, by the horrible water he had been compelled to drink while leading his troops—"the worst water," he calls it, " ever drunk by an army, which even my horse refused with a shudder of disgust." It is true that in March 1849 he got as far as Agra, on his way to the Punjâb; but the war was then just over, and he was ordered back to his post, and, eight months later, was once more back in England, where he joined his wife and family, who had left India in April. Havelock had been ordered home on account of his health; but not getting better at Plymouth, he went in the spring to Germany, examining on his way, with a soldier's eye, the field of Waterloo. The following winter he was back in

London, and, after another summer abroad, he turned his face once more eastward, reaching India, with renewed health, in December 1851.

A few peaceful years followed, but they were very lonely ones, for, not yet feeling sure of his health, he was afraid to send for his wife, lest he should have to return again to England. And it was well his family did not come out; for troubles were gathering in the future, and in the midst of the horrors of the Indian Mutiny, he must often have been thankful that his dear ones were safely sheltered.

But before Havelock went forth to the war that has made his name so famous, there was fighting to be done in Persia. A fresh quarrel had broken out about Herat. Persian troops had seized the city, and war was declared. British war-ships sailed out of Bombay, across the Indian Ocean, up the Persian Gulf, and landed their troops at Bushire, not very far from the mouth of the great Euphrates. Next day a battle was fought, and the town captured, without a single man of the British force being killed.

But Havelock had not then reached Persia. Sir James Outram, of whom we shall hear more presently, was to command the whole army, and he started with the second division, having sent for Havelock to command it. Havelock was at Agra, and although he travelled at breakneck speed to Bombay, getting upset on the road, and arriving at the end of his journey with a black eye, Outram had sailed without him, and another battle had been fought before he reached Persian shores.

Steamers carried the troops up the mouth of the Euphrates, and, on the 24th of March 1857, the fortifications of Mohumra came in sight, peeping out from beautiful date-groves. Early on the 26th the great cannon from the British war-ships threw shot and shell into the fort, till the Persians ceased firing and our troops could land. While the troops were leaving the vessels, a powder magazine in Mohumra blew up, throwing the Persians into greater confusion than ever; so that, when Havelock led his men up through the waving palm trees to the enemy's camp, he found it empty and deserted, the enemy having fled in panic. A few horse soldiers were sent in pursuit; and three days after, when our troops sailed a hundred miles up the river, seven thousand Persians ran away as hard as they could go before three hundred British soldiers, without stopping to fire a shot.

Peace was now signed, and the war was over. Havelock was sorry. He writes: " I never felt better in my life, and though I am sixty-two I can campaign as merrily as I could ten years ago, and shall be quite ready for China when this is over." It was well his health and spirits were so good; he would need the very best of both now for the most important work of his life.

But not in China. A fearful storm was brewing nearer at hand, and though no one then suspected danger, it would very soon burst with terrible fury upon the peaceful provinces in which Havelock had long made his home.

CHAPTER VI.

THE REBEL SEPOY.

IF you were to offer a Hindu a few gold pieces as
a reward, he would cheerfully spit in the face of
the idol he worships, curse it, or pitch it into the
river, or even sit down and write a book to prove
that his religion is all lies; but if you offered him a
thousand gold pieces he would never touch his lips
with beef, nor indeed eat food of any kind if you
had handled the plate on which it was served up, or
had come too near while it was being cooked. This
man's "caste" is much more precious in his eyes than
anything else, and he will go perfectly frantic if he
thinks it is in danger. The highest of the four castes
among the Hindus is that of the Brahmin. Mohammedans, of whom there are great numbers in India,
are divided into classes much like castes, and they
would on no account eat a morsel of pork, for they
consider the pig an unclean animal, while the Hindus
regard the cow as sacred.

Now, of course, it would be quite impossible for us
to spare enough soldiers from England to defend
India; and, besides this, English soldiers are much
tried by the fierce heat of an Indian sun. So we
have trained great numbers of natives, and set English
commanders over them. These native soldiers are
Hindus and Mohammedans, and, whatever else they
might give up, they would never give up their caste.

With so many natives in our army in India, it
was very important that they should be obedient to

their English masters; that they should have perfect confidence in us, because they were well treated; and also that they should be a *little* afraid of us. And at one time the sepoys, or native soldiers, both trusted our promises and feared our power. But in 1856 their confidence in our word and their respect for our valour were both sadly weakened. Most unfortunately, in 1852, Lord Dalhousie ordered out to Burmah a sepoy regiment that had been engaged for service only in Hindustan. The men were very indignant, actually refusing to go on board ship, and they were allowed to remain in India.

Now, for a soldier to refuse to obey orders is a very serious matter indeed, and such disobedience is usually most severely punished; for there would be no possibility of victory, or even of safety, if it were allowed. The sepoys thought, therefore, that their masters were not to be trusted if they broke promises; and also, that it was possible to do as they liked without being punished. Our troubles and losses, too, in Afghanistan were not forgotten, for they proved that British soldiers *could* be defeated; and rumours about our disasters in the Crimea also reached India. It happened that a young man from the court of Nana Sahib, an Indian prince, was staying in England, and heard all about the terrible slaughter in the trenches of Sebastopol. This story he related to his master, who concluded that the English were just about to be utterly crushed, and now was the time to rise in rebellion and put an end to British rule, especially as one of the Indian prophets had declared that the " Feringhee " would only hold India for one hundred years, and that period was just expiring.

An idea, too, was spreading among the sepoys that their masters meant to convert them all to Christianity by force, by destroying their caste. This made them very angry, though they carefully concealed their ill-feeling beneath an appearance of goodwill and respect; and this they did so successfully that almost every English officer had *perfect* confidence in his men, and was quite sure that whatever *other* regiments might do, *his* would always be loyal. The governors, too, imagined the empire to be in perfect repose. But all the while a spirit of rebellion was spreading over the country, and the leaders among the sepoys, who thought they could soon overthrow British power if they could only arrange a general rising, found it very easy to arouse discontent and hatred among the men, and to induce them to believe any stories, however false, against their rulers.

Just at this time a new weapon was being put into the hands of the sepoys. The Enfield rifle was a great improvement on the old-fashioned musket; but the cartridge with which it was loaded was smeared with fat, and this the soldier would have to bite or tear with his teeth. A cartridge is a charge of powder wrapped in paper. Now the sepoy was horrified at the idea of touching this fat; for would it not destroy his caste and render him unclean? The alarm spread like wildfire through the army, for the Asiatic never stops to listen to reason. He is like an angry child, too excited and passionate to hear any explanation. It was in vain that the officers tried to soothe the men, assuring them that the fat used was not that of pigs or cows; or that, if they thought it was, they were not compelled to bite it, and, indeed, might grease their cartridges themselves. The sepoys still nursed their indignation, and only waited the signal of their leaders to rise in rebellion.

And if this signal had been given at the same time all over the country, and the natives had replied to it at once, while the British Government was entirely unprepared, very possibly we might not have been holding India to-day. But, happily, this was not done ; neither did the native population ever take much part in the insurrection, except to plunder and murder where they thought they could do it safely ; indeed, the rebellion is almost always called the " Mutiny," because it was mostly confined to the army.

The first signs of ill-feeling showed themselves as early as February 1857, while Havelock was still in Persia. Some natives broke out against British authority at Berhampore, and, unfortunately, the Government did not see the coming danger, or understand that thousands of other sepoys were ready to do what these had done. The punishment for mutiny is death, and though it seems very hard to say so, these rebels ought to have been all shot. The execution of fifty soldiers at that moment, horrible as it would have been, would most likely have saved thousands of lives.

Terrible news awaited Havelock when he reached Bombay on the 29th of May. Nearly three weeks before, mutiny and bloodshed had broken in on the peace of the Sunday evening at Meerut, a town to the north-east of Delhi. No one suspected harm. Evening worship was just beginning, when the sepoys sud-

denly seized their arms, shot down some of their
officers, marched to the jail and liberated their companions, and then fell upon and murdered many
Europeans. The rebels then started for Delhi, one of
the most important towns in India ; for it is not only
very large and strongly defended by massive walls,
but it contained in 1857 an immense supply of
weapons, gunpowder, and food, was garrisoned by a
large force of natives, and was inhabited by a great
number of Europeans. This city, then, the rebels
were anxious to secure as their stronghold. Unhappily, they found little difficulty in doing so, no
attempt being made to stop their march, although
this might easily have been done had European troops
followed them up promptly.

And when the sepoys reached Delhi, the city gates
were thrown open by traitors. Not a single European
regiment had been left in charge of this most important post, and the sepoys whose duty it was to
guard the palace belonged to that very regiment that
had defied orders when commanded to embark for
Burmah. Some Europeans did their best to defend
the Bank ; but it was taken, and all its defenders
killed ; while the powder magazine was blown into the
air by the English to save it from the rebels. Then
followed dreadful scenes of murder, robbery, and destruction by fire. A great many Europeans escaped,
but all the rest were slaughtered—at least all that
could be found ; a few hid themselves and thus escaped
the cruel swords.

When they had possessed themselves of the city,
the sepoys brought out the old king of Delhi, who
still lived there, and set him up for their monarch, as

Emperor of India. It is not at all certain that the king approved of this return to sovereignty—most likely he was afraid that it would, in the end, cost him his head—but he was in the power of the soldiers, and had to do as they liked. Very soon other regiments in the neighbourhood behaved as those at Meerut had done, and having killed or driven away their officers, marched to Delhi, till there were 20,000 rebels within its walls. Indeed, all the way down the Ganges to Allahabad, a district inhabited by thirty millions of people, there was no sign at all of British authority, except at Agra, and in the feeble intrenchment at Cawnpore, which was surrounded by bloodthirsty foes.

Such was the story hurriedly related to Havelock on his return to India; a story which, until he had put many anxious questions, he could hardly bring himself to believe. But, horrible as it was, he could not idly stand still, shocked and stunned at the tidings. Embarking again at once, he sailed for Calcutta, to take orders from the Commander-in-Chief, and be ready to march against the rebels; for he well knew that so long as they held Delhi, British rule in India was in the greatest peril, and that before long not only all the country round the Ganges would be full of mutiny, but the Punjâb would also rise, and, perhaps, bring on disaster which could never be repaired. On reaching Calcutta, Havelock was at once sent off to Allahabad, Cawnpore, and Lucknow, though his Commander-in-Chief little guessed at the moment what a tremendous task he was setting the brave general, or how long it would be before it could be accomplished. "Go and put down all disorder first at Allahabad, and then be ready to help Sir Hugh Wheeler at Cawnpore and Sir Henry Lawrence at Lucknow. Scatter and destroy as you go all sepoys who have mutinied, and, above all, *be quick about it !*"

Such were the orders Havelock received, and at once he hastened to obey. But, happily, help had come to Allahabad before this, or the rebels would have established themselves in that town as securely as in Delhi. An officer named Neill had come into Calcutta about a month before at the head of a fine regiment known as "The Lambs," though the men more resembled *lions* in their courage and daring. He had not been in the city a day before some of his "Lambs" were started up the Ganges. Anxious to despatch more by railway, and there being no train ready, he simply took possession of one in the station, filled it with his troops, and forced the driver to start express for Benares, the most sacred city of India, which at this moment was in great danger. Neill arrived just in time; poured a tremendous fire among the mutinous sepoys; hanged men right and left for treason as fast as he caught them; and so thoroughly terrified the rebels, that their power was broken and order was restored. Thus a fearful scene of massacre was prevented by the prompt, ready action of a single man, who did not fear to do what appeared desperate, and to do it at once when he saw there was real need.

After this Neill hurried off to Allahabad, where, a day or two before, a sepoy regiment had murdered fourteen of its officers, broken open the prison, and set fire to the houses. Now it happened, just then, that some more men of this regiment were guarding the gate of the fortress, which in a few moments they would have thrown open to the rebels. But a sergeant, who must have been made of much the same stuff as Colonel Neill, saved it. Brasyer was commanding some Sikhs, and an officer who had escaped the slaughter galloped up and ordered him to turn out his regiment instantly, and overpower the treacherous sepoys, taking away their arms. Now the Sikhs were faithful to us all through the Mutiny, though sometimes it seemed doubtful if they could be trusted; and just now this particular regiment seemed very discontented, and by no means inclined to obey orders. Brasyer knew that if they did *not* obey, Allahabad would be in the rebels' hands, and, like Neill, he determined to have his way. Seizing a red-hot iron he stood over the gunpowder store, and declared that if the men did not *instantly* obey him he would blow the whole regiment up in the sky. Before such a threat the men gave way abashed; the sepoys were disarmed and the fortress was saved—at all events till Neill's "Lambs" could arrive and offer further help. Through fearful heat the little company, with their brave leader, pressed forward on foot, seven out of the forty falling by sunstroke on the road, and Neill himself so dead-beat that his men had to throw water over him to keep him on his feet at all. The rebels, however, soon gave way when the resolute little force came up; plunder and destruction ceased, and the rascals fled like whipped puppies before the relentless fire that swept them out of the city.

But if Allahabad was thus, by the most desperate measures, restored to order, and British authority

once more established, it was impossible to reach
Cawnpore and Lucknow, each more than a hundred
miles away, in time to save them from being entirely
hemmed in by cruel foes.   The railway had been
entirely destroyed; fifteen hundred bullocks, collected
for dragging cannon and waggons, had been driven
off; and cholera broke out among the British troops.
Nevertheless Neill worked away as hard as ever.
He knew that Havelock, not himself, would have the
command of the expedition; but no selfish pride
damped his ardour, and he busied himself collecting
food, waggons, and bullocks for the use of the general's expected brigade.   Early on the 30th Havelock
arrived, and on the 7th of July the army set forward.
A small force had gone on a little in advance, but
when the two united there were not more than nine-
teen hundred men to meet many thousands of rebels,
and of this number only fourteen hundred were
British soldiers.

At first there had been every hope of saving the
brave garrison besieged in Cawnpore, but before
Havelock's army set out very bad news came in to
Allahabad.   All the garrison, so it was reported, were
destroyed, and the city was in the enemy's hands,
though many women and children still lived.   But it
was impossible to know whether this story was true;
the rebels might have concocted it on purpose to dis-
courage the British troops from hurrying forward.
Neill, at all events, thought the story only a false
alarm; and although Havelock sent word to Major
Renaud, who was with the regiment in advance, to be
cautious how he moved forward, nothing was allowed
to hinder the immediate start of the rest of the army,

many of the men, for whom suitable clothing could not be obtained, marching under a burning sun in woollen tunics.

But while Havelock and his men press on over the scorching sands in uncertainty and dread, we will go forward to Cawnpore and inquire whether the dreadful tidings be really true.

CHAPTER VII.

THE STORY OF CAWNPORE.

ON the banks of the Ganges, and in the very heart of Northern India, nearly six hundred miles from Calcutta, stands the city of Cawnpore; but, although an important military station, and occupied by a number of English, there were, in 1857, only a very few British soldiers inside its walls, although it contained three thousand sepoys.

The general, Sir Hugh Wheeler, had commanded native troops for more than fifty years, and, in spite of ill news of mutiny, could hardly believe it possible that these soldiers, whom he had so often led to victory, could possibly prove unfaithful. Besides this, the native prince at Bithoor, Nana Sahib, had always professed the utmost friendliness, and he had immense influence with the natives. Still, Sir Hugh could not help noticing signs of discontent, and thought it might be wise to provide for the safety of the women and children *in case* of any outbreak. Unfortunately, he chose as a place of refuge some barracks formerly used as a soldiers' hospital, the walls of which were very thin and the roof thatched with straw. Round this building he had a low mud wall built, or, as soldiers would call it, an "intrenchment," enough provisions being stored within to last twenty-five days.

On the night of the 4th of June, while Havelock had not yet reached Calcutta, the sepoys at Cawnpore broke out into mutiny. Nana Sahib, instead of defending the British, as he had promised to do, took part with the rebels, and persuaded them not to march to Delhi as the others had done, but to stay and secure Cawnpore. They had then left the city, and the British, hoping they had finally gone, were intending to escape down the Ganges to Allahabad; but, alas! the faithless Nana Sahib sent word that he meant to attack the British garrison at once. All huddled into the intrenchment and prepared to defend it, and before the solemn words of prayer were concluded with which the chaplain commended the dauntless little company into their Father's hands, the smoke of burning villages could be seen in the distance, and the rattle of firearms and the roar of furious men reached the ears of the terrified women and children. But worse was to follow. Very soon bullets fell like hail, and one by one the brave defenders were struck down at their post, while women endured the torture of seeing their loved ones die with little or no means of dressing their wounds or relieving their sufferings.

And as the weary days of agony went by, many little children drooped, and faded, and died. Shut up in close, unhealthy air, terrified at the fearful sights of bloodshed around them, and breaking their mothers' hearts by pleading for the milk that it was impossible to give, the little ones became the first victims among the miserable garrison. No little flower-crowned coffin could be carried lovingly to its last resting-place in the quiet churchyard. Just outside the intrenchment there was an empty well. To approach this by day would have been certain death; but, as night fell, and firing gradually ceased, a few stalwart men would creep cautiously out, carrying on litters the dead bodies of those who had fallen during the day. Down into the gloomy well the sad burdens were dropped; and at the end of the siege, this dreadful sepulchre held two hundred and fifty British dead. Better had it held them all, for over another well close by is written a yet more tragic story.

But it is not alone of suffering and starvation and death that we think, in looking back to the time of that terrible siege, for it is a "*glorious*" as well as a "piteous story." Gallant deeds of cool, unrewarded heroism were wrought during those awful three weeks; deeds that ought to make us proud of the name of Briton, and careful that we never sully it by any unworthy action. Not only was the miserable little intrenchment stoutly defended against thousands of rebels, but those among the men who could not fight were no less prepared to risk their lives in loyal service for others. Water could only be obtained at the price of blood, for upon the one well that supplied the garrison there rained down an almost unceasing shower of bullets from the besiegers. Many a brave man gave his life that the parched lips of thirsty little ones and fainting women might be refreshed with a cool draught of water, and a hero named John Mackillop took the perilous post of captain of the well until stricken down by the murderous fire. We must remember, too, that it was entirely for the sake of the women and children that men fought and suffered thus. Had they been alone, or had it been possible for Britons to think of leaving helpless ones to their fate, the soldiers could have cut their way out, and though some must have fallen, many would have escaped with their lives.

And it was also for the sake of the women and children that surrender was at last consented to. Nana Sahib offered to provide boats and convey them all in safety to Allahabad, if the British gave up the town. Such an offer on their own behalf these noble fellows would have scorned, much preferring to die fighting bravely to the last; but it was too pitiful to see the weak and the tender suffer as they did, and suffer with such patient, pathetic heroism. The proposals of the rebels were therefore listened to; terms were made; and, with the boats waiting but a mile away, the forlorn band set out, as they thought, toward safety and peace.

It was a motley, miserable crowd. Gaunt, sunburnt, weary, but still resolute soldiers; huge elephants; litters, on which were stretched the sick and the wounded; well-born ladies, pale and exhausted, yet their faces alight with a faint glow of hope, and carrying in their arms such of their little ones who still remained alive,—all these trooped out of the city and down to the river-banks. Alas! that peaceful river was soon to run red with British blood. No sooner were all the company on board, than the treacherous

Nana Sahib, who seems to have been more a demon than a human being, called upon his men to fire upon those whom he had sworn, by the most solemn oaths, to protect, and who had been, unhappily, too ready to trust his word. So fiendishly cruel did this monster of wickedness prove a few weeks later, that it would have been well had this awful scene of butchery continued till not a single Briton was left alive.

But this was not to be. "Stay," cried the fickle tyrant, when the banks and the waters were strown with dead—"stay, I will have no more killing to-day, though I do not intend to let one Feringhee go free. Take all that are alive and lead them back prisoners into the city to await my royal pleasure, for *I* am master now; and when we have made an end of the Feringhees here, I shall march my conquering armies to possess Allahabad, and then move on in triumph to Calcutta."

So the wretched captives were collected, half-stupified at the awful scene around them, dripping from the water, stained with blood; while many were almost maddened at the loss of husbands, wives, or little ones shot down before their eyes. Sweet hope had gone forth with the heroic band that left Cawnpore: the darkest despair weighed down the hearts of the few poor captives who returned. First came a party of women and children, some almost stripped, others barefoot; all the men had been killed in their defence. An hour after followed a boatload that had got away during the first attack, but, after a furious defence on the part of the gallant soldiers it contained, had fallen into the hands of its foes. When the dismal procession reached the city, Nana Sahib ordered all the men (about sixty) to be separated from the women and shot. "Then I will die with my husband!" exclaimed an English lady, springing to her husband's side and refusing to leave him. "So will we!" replied all the others, and it was in vain that the brave men, in their last extremity, implored their beloved ones to leave them and accept safety, at least for the present. "No, we will die together!" said they, sobbing in their husbands' arms, till at last the rough, brutal murderers tore them away by force, and a volley of musket shot told them they were all widows!

There were now only two hundred of the garrison left alive, and these were all women and children. "Take them in there," said the haughty tyrant, pointing to a low bungalow, or Indian house, sheltered by trees. Into this little building, therefore, were huddled the whole of the miserable company, half-dead with fright and fatigue, many badly wounded, and all oppressed with a sickening dread of what might be yet to follow.

There we must leave them awhile, and go back to see what progress Havelock is making with his gallant troops in pressing forward to their rescue.

CHAPTER VIII.

TOO LATE!

"I HAVE lived to command in a successful action." So wrote Havelock to his wife after the first battle fought on the way to Cawnpore. On starting from Allahabad, the troops had gone forward by easy marches, only doing eight miles a day, though this, we must remember, was either through torrents of tropical rain or under the blazing beams of an Indian sun, at a time of year when the life of no white man was safe if he ventured out at noonday. After parade in the cool of the early dawn, no British soldier in India, in times of peace, is called out again till sunset.

But the perils of sunstroke, fever, and cholera were as little regarded by these brave men as were the sepoy bullets; for were not their countrymen, and worse still, their *countrywomen*, in danger? No risk was therefore too great to be run for the chance of saving them. Many of the men in Havelock's little force were his old friends; he had led them in Persia, and knew, as he said, "the stuff they were made of." The Ross-shire Buffs, Highlanders, are some of the most splendid fighters in the British army.

Their general had now secured the position he had so long desired, being placed in command of the expedition. By this time Havelock was one of the most experienced soldiers in India, and though sixty-two years of age, as fit for the field as at forty. Erect, slim in figure, with hair whitened in long service, but with the penetrating glance of his quick eye as keen as ever, he rode at the head of his troops, proud to command such a noble band of men, and resolute in purpose to lead them on to victory. And the beloved commander of "Havelock's saints" was still holding fast to his love and reverence for that God who had led him all his life long to this day, and placed him, at last, in a position where he would be able to render such brilliant service to his country; for he undertook his important mission as from the hand of Jehovah, and in the hour of victory acknowledged that success was due not merely to the new Enfield rifle in British hands, nor to unfailing British "pluck," but to "the blessing of Almighty God on the cause of justice, humanity, truth, and good government in India."

On the evening of the 11th of July the main army overtook the little force that had been sent forward some time before Havelock started. Renaud, its commander, was thankful to welcome his friends, for some Cawnpore rebels, finding that his numbers were very small, were marching down to attack him. The whole army, therefore, moved forward sixteen miles during the night, and, before breakfast in the morning, fought a battle with the sepoys, forcing them back into the town of Futtehpore. This was the first victory in a field-fight since the outbreak of the Mutiny; and while it warned the rebels that the Feringhee was not to be driven from the country so easily as they had imagined, it put fresh heart into the British everywhere, and began to make Havelock's name famous in his native land.

Futtehpore was burned, and the next great struggle took place at the bridge of Aong, a few miles farther on. There were no boats by which to cross, and the river was far too deep to ford, so it would never do to let the enemy either keep possession of the bridge or destroy it. Once more, then, hungry men left their meal untouched and hurried forward to the attack. And it was a pretty hot one, for the sepoys were by no means willing to give up their position, and at one time, a flash, and a puff, and a roar made them fear they had blown up the bridge. But although the rebels had attempted this, they had not laid their charge of powder rightly, and but little damage was done. The British force rested that night a mile on the other side of the river, the enemy being in full retreat. But it was a comfortless repose, for no tents had arrived, and the cattle came up so late that, when they were killed, the men were too weary to cook the meat, and it was all spoiled during the sultry night.

Before dawn, every man was again in the ranks, fatigue, wounds, and hunger all forgotten ; for had not their brave hearts been stirred by the words of their chief, as, with bared head and drawn sword, he had told them that two hundred captive women and children yet remained alive in Cawnpore ? " With God's help," shouted Havelock, " we shall save them, or every man of us die in the attempt ! I am trying you sorely, men, I know," he added, " but I have seen what you can do. Think of our women and their tender infants in the power of savage brutes ! "

There was no need to sound an " Advance " after that. With ringing cheers the men pressed forward, and, without a murmur, plodded on through that burning day, some of them till they positively could not go another step, and fell dead or dying on the roadway. To Havelock's great regret the store of *rum* was now running low, and he was most anxious to obtain more to supply the men with full rations of " grog ; " for although he remembered how much better his troops had worked in Jelalabad when unable to get any liquor, he had no idea that the abstinence which had been such a blessing during the bitter cold of an Afghan winter would be of equal benefit under the scorching sun of an Indian summer. But so it proved; rum was far out of reach, and many a brave soldier's life was saved that would otherwise have been sacrificed.

No less a foe than the infamous murderer Nana Sahib himself met the British force as it approached Cawnpore. Driven from his other positions, he had collected here some five thousand men to defy "the army of the living God." And Havelock was duly warned of his presence. Two sepoys, faithful amid a host of rebels, came into the camp with tidings of the *utmost* value to the English commander; for they explained exactly how the Indian chief had arranged his troops, and how, therefore, he could be attacked with the greatest hope of success.

To silence the enemy's cannon by our own fire seemed hopeless, and at Havelock's word Hamilton led on the Ross-shire Buffs to the charge, while the weird music of the bagpipe, so sweet to the Scottish ear, mingled with the shrill Highland war-cry. And nothing could stand against those fellows when their blood was up. Down went the sepoy gunners, ramrod in hand, dead at their post; down went the regiment behind them, for there was no time to fly; away scampered the rebels in the rear in wild, headlong confusion. The guns were taken, the village was cleared, the defence at that point utterly broken up; but still the brave Highlanders had more work in hand. Havelock himself summoned them. "Now, Highlanders," he cried, "another charge like that wins the day." Pointing to a big cannon pouring forth fire and death, he galloped at the head of his men to the charge. The cannon was taken; the enemy again repulsed; and after a further march of about a mile, and the capture of another village, the wearied soldiers hoped to rest for the night, all resistance appearing to be over for the present.

But even yet their work was not done. Coming to the top of a little slope quite near the gates of the city, they suddenly beheld a sight which would have made less resolute hearts quake, while bullets whizzed about their heads, and more than one man fell, wounded and bleeding. A herd of rebels swarmed right across the road, while fresh troops poured forth from the gate, a roar of scornful shouts and the sound of native music mingling with the roll of drums and the notes of the bugle. In their midst, mounted on a magnificent elephant decked with gay trappings and glittering with gold and jewels, moved the vile and savage murderer of helpless women, Nana Sahib, hoping to encourage his men to make a last successful resistance to the oncoming of the avenger. "Lie down!" rang out the officers' command to each regiment. This saved the men, for the moment, from the terrible hail of bullets, for our cannon were far behind, and night was coming on.

But lying down and waiting would not win the day; there was nothing for it but another charge. Havelock, whose horse had been shot under him, rode to the front on a pony. "The longer you look at it, men," said he, "the less you will like it. Rise up! The brigade will advance!"

None knew better than their general what such an order would cost. Death must meet many of the bravest of the brave in that fearful charge, but to delay or to waver might result in the whole army being scattered or cut to pieces. Forward they went, those valorous, determined Highlanders, greeted by showers of grape-shot from the enemy's guns. Twenty —thirty—forty fell from the 64th Regiment, leaving its path strewed with wounded and dying. But wounds and death could not stay the steady, silent progress of men who knew that behind that line of murderous fire were pent up frail and suffering women at the mercy of fiends. As they drew nearer, a wild, piercing cheer rent the air, and in another moment they were upon the foe, cutting down the gunners at their post, and sending the baffled host flying in hopeless disorder.

Victory now was in their hands at last, but only the morning light could reveal what that victory had bought. Supperless, the men sank to sleep on the bare ground, Havelock with bridle on arm in case of sudden surprise, and with no refreshment but a single biscuit and some porter. The bugler at his side, with much of the cool spirit of the true soldier, quietly announced the exact time (two hours and three-quarters) that it had taken to fight their way to the city gates.

Alas, that noble conflict and that weary night were followed by a sad awakening! When the early bugle aroused the troops, a dreadful whisper of evil tidings ran through the lines: the women and children for whom they had fought and suffered and died were all brutally *murdered!*

The city being deserted, it was easy to march in at once, and search out the truth of the awful story. The Savada House, where the rebel prince had been living, had evidently been occupied a few hours before. While the soldiers were exploring its garden, where a handsome tent had been pitched, and where also, to their horror, they found the dead body of an English girl, the last salute of the enemy broke on their ears. It was the roar of the powder magazine, blown into the air by the retreating rebel troops. But when they enter the city a sight meets their eyes from which even those rough, hardy men turn away with a shudder of agony. The streets are silent and empty, except where, here and there, a dark form creeps away cowering at the sight of the victorious English. Presently a few soldiers approach that flat-roofed bungalow where we saw Nana Sahib shut in his helpless captives. Ah, why is the grass so trampled? What mean those dark stains on the path, those scraps of scattered lace, that fragment of a tiny white frock? With stern faces, but silent lips, the men press on. No tearful sob of welcome, no music of children's voices, for the hope of which they had forced their way through fire and blood, falls on their ears. All is still with the dreadful silence of the grave, but none of its peace. One of the soldiers crosses the threshold, but though he can face unflinchingly the stream of death at the cannon's mouth, or the sight of the dead on the battle-field, he cannot face this. He staggers back to his companions, who read in his face the awful story. Yet not a single dead body lies within those walls. Only the blood-marked floor, the torn dress, the broken toy, the little pinafore all stained and slashed, the golden curl, the crushed and scattered ornaments, the tattered letter, the baby's shoe, —only these are left to tell of the most horrid and cowardly massacre ever seen under God's blue heaven.

And Nana Sahib had done it all! Unable to conquer his dauntless enemy in fair fight, he had turned, villain that he was, upon the helpless ones in his power. "Fire on them! Kill them all!" rang out the inhuman command. To the everlasting honour of a band of rebel sepoys, who, reckless as they were, shrank from such infamy as this, they refused to obey orders, and Nana's guards, together with butchers from the streets, were summoned to carry out the will of the bloodthirsty tyrant. And out there in the courtyard, thrust in hideous confusion into the deep well, and filling it to the brim, lay two hundred bodies of innocent women and children—a sight from which the very horses recoiled with a shiver of horror.

Can we wonder that a group of these stern soldiers, who held the life of the weak and the helpless as a sacred thing, should have gathered up a beautiful golden tress from some fair head, and, counting over each hair, have sworn that a rebel should die for every one of them!

CHAPTER IX.

VALOUR AND VICTORY.

SAD, dispiriting days followed the capture of Cawnpore. There were many wounded to be cared for, many dead to be buried; cholera broke out in the camp; fierce foes, though driven out of the city, were still close at hand, and the sad tidings arrived of the death of Sir Henry Lawrence, in command at Lucknow.

But if Havelock was very anxious just now, and very exhausted, too, by all the hardships he had undergone, he allowed nothing to stand in the way of an immediate attempt to reach the besieged city Colonel Neill now came up with over two hundred men, and was left in charge of Cawnpore with its sick and wounded, while the general crossed the Ganges, and hastened on toward Lucknow. But there was another river to cross, the bridge of which was held by Nana Sahib; and also the canal at Lucknow Battle after battle was fought in the desperate attempt to go forward. But the men were dying of cholera; the heat was intense; the hope of the arrival of fresh troops was disappointed; Neill was in danger at Cawnpore, and, therefore, to his great regret, Havelock was obliged to turn back, recross the Ganges, and after scattering the enemy, who had collected again at Bithoor, wait for Sir James Outram's force before again setting forward.

This retreat, though it brought no glory, was an act of real heroism, for it proved that the general could *wait* as well as *fight*, and that he would not lose the chance of completing the work before him by any foolhardy exploit, however splendid or valorous. But while waiting at Cawnpore, news came to hand that would have dismayed a less lofty spirit. Sir James Outram was appointed to the command, and on his arrival Havelock would have to obey orders again, instead of being his own master. The appointment was not an unjust one, and Havelock knew it, and wisely prepared himself to take his new position in good part. On the 1st of September Outram reached Allahabad with the troops sent on by Sir

Colin Campbell, the Commander-in-Chief. Havelock, while he waited, was quite unmolested at Cawnpore. But bad news came from Lucknow, for Inglis, who had succeeded Lawrence, found it very hard to hold out against the continual storm of shot and shell, and he had a large number of sick, as well as women and children, to protect. It was, therefore, with almost feverish impatience that, on the arrival of Outram and his force, Havelock crossed the Ganges once more on the 19th of September, and set forward, for every day of inaction gave opportunity to the rebels to strengthen their position and spread mutiny wider over the land. "I consider," wrote Havelock, "that the whole Bengal army *has* mutinied, that the Bombay *will*, and that the Madras has a good mind to."

But Havelock crossed the river *still* as the leader of the whole army; for Outram had generously refused to take the command out of his hands until he had reaped the fruit of his long toil and suffering in the joy and honour of succouring his besieged countrymen in Lucknow. No sooner was the river crossed than there was more fighting to do, though the scene of three fights in the first advance, Busseerutgunge, was passed through now without difficulty, and the bridge over the Sye River was found still uninjured.

On the 23rd the army came up to the Alumbagh, a beautiful pleasure-garden on the borders of Lucknow, which had to be fought for before it was possible to approach the city. But, in spite of a furious defence, every cannon was taken, and every rebel either killed or put to flight. Just as Outram was returning from the last pursuit of the enemy, his life having been twice saved during the fight by Havelock's son Henry, a letter was put into his hands containing welcome news which gladdened every heart:—*Delhi was taken from the rebels;* and the weary, hungry men cheered lustily before they lay down to snatch a little rest on the soaking ground.

But it was harder to fight in streets and squares than in the open field. The British force in Lucknow had never been able to hold the town. On the outbreak of the Mutiny, they had retreated into the Residency, a group of houses belonging to Europeans, the principal one being that of the Governor, Sir Henry Lawrence. Here they had gallantly fought for their lives day by day, for they were surrounded by savage foes, and had no fort or strong protection of any kind.

The first thing, then, to be done was to force a passage into the town—a most difficult and perilous task, for six cannon poured their fire across the bridge, and high houses on either side were filled with armed men. The attack was made on the 25th, and Havelock, rising before dawn, spent some time in earnest prayer before going forth to face possible wounds and death in the desperate encounter.

The sick and wounded men were, of course, left behind under safe guard at the Alumbagh when the troops set out for the bridge. The first efforts to dislodge the foe were quite unavailing. The gunners at the only two cannon for which there was room were shot down, so with a wild rush young Havelock, followed by several other officers and a little band of men, charged across the bridge into the very jaws of death. *Every one* except young Havelock fell; but the next moment the "Lambs" followed headlong

over the dead bodies of their comrades, and, before
the rebel cannon could be reloaded, leaped the barricade,
struck down every gunner at his post, and won the
bridge.   Immediately the whole army poured into the
city; not to advance far, however, without leaving
many dead in their path, for a terrible fire rained
down upon them from every window and roof.   Just
after the bridge was taken young Havelock fell,
wounded in the arm, and was carried forward insens-
ible.   Neill, too, fell just in the moment of triumph;
in passing through a narrow archway a shot from a
rebel's hand close by killed him instantly.

The gate of the Residency was now in sight, and
the shouts of the garrison could be distinctly heard.
The troops, mindful of their disappointment at Cawnpore, were eager for the last desperate rush, that they
might clasp the hands of those whom they had fought
so hard to save; therefore, although Outram, anxious
to spare his men, urged a halt, to allow some regiments behind to come up, Havelock led them forward
at once.   It was a tremendous struggle, but Highlanders, who led the way, never yield when once their
face is turned to the foe.   On they went.   Showers
of whizzing bullets, stones and furniture hurled from
the houses, deep trenches cut in the road,—all alike
failed to stay the progress of men pressing to the
relief of their imprisoned, perhaps famishing, comrades,
and whose hearts bled still when they recalled the
memory of that awful well at Cawnpore.

And it was a welcome worth fighting for.   Outram
was the first inside; not through the gate, it is true,
for that had been so banked up with earth that it
was impossible to open it.   A great cannon, which

had done good service, showed its threatening muzzle through a ragged hole in the wall. This was hauled back from within, and Outram attempted to leap through the opening on his huge charger. The horse hung back, but a party of stout Highlanders made short work of hoisting horse and rider right over the bit of broken wall. The next moment Havelock followed; a crowd of eager soldiers pouring in after him, covered with dust, blackened with powder, stained with blood, but cheering to the echo, and, while they seized the hands of their comrades in a transport of joy, many a rough face was also wet with tears. Out flocked the ladies among the grim warriors, giving them their hands to kiss—yes, and flinging their arms about their necks in grateful gladness; while the soldiers seemed as though they would never be satisfied with the sweetness of feeling the soft warm hands of the little ones stroking their hard faces and shaggy beards, or of hearing the ravishing music of prattling voices, for which they had fought and suffered in vain on the plain of Cawnpore. From the hospital the wounded crawled out to join in the glad welcome—a welcome which their deliverers had fought twelve battles to enjoy, and lost one out of every three men in their ranks. And the remembrance of their dead threw a mournful shadow over even this hour of rejoicing; for as the men accepted the much-needed food eagerly prepared for them, they sadly inquired of each other the names of missing comrades.

On the 26th Outram took up the command which he had so nobly left in Havelock's hands till after the relief of the garrison, and Havelock undertook, at his direction, the task of driving out the enemy from the palaces and houses on the road. This was done in a few days, and the Highlanders, after their supperless nights on the wet ground, now took their meals out of costly dishes, and rested on gay, silken sofas. But to get *into* Lucknow was one thing, to get *out* quite another. Fortunately, the store of food was much larger than had been supposed; for it was impossible to remove the women and children in safety until more soldiers should arrive to protect them. At present even the few troops left at the Alumbagh were out of reach. Very little could, therefore, be done until the arrival of Sir Colin Campbell on the 10th of November. The Commander-in-Chief had a hard fight to make his way through, but on the 17th the three generals met. Havelock narrowly escaped with his life, a shell bursting at his feet. He was thrown down, but quite uninjured, and, scrambling up, rushed across a stream of bullets to a place of safety. His son was wounded a second time in the left arm on this eventful day, and a plucky young aide-de-camp, who was very much attached to General Havelock, rode twice across that same stream of fire to find out the nature of the wound and relieve the father's anxiety.

The title of "Sir Henry" was now bestowed on the gallant general; but, alas! he was not long to enjoy it, or even to know that his grateful country also made him a baronet, and gave him a pension of a thousand a year. Although he had received no wound, these months of hardship had tried the old veteran sorely, and, while his soldiers little guessed the sad truth, his days of marching and of fighting were ended. On the 19th, Havelock wrote cheerfully to his wife, venturing to hope for a safe return now that the worst of the fighting was over.

But what bullet and bayonet had left undone, disease accomplished. Those two months in the Lucknow Residency, breathing the poisonous air of the hospitals and living on unwholesome and scanty food, brought down the strength of the grand old warrior to a very low ebb; for though Havelock was but sixty-two, few Englishmen are able to bear active service in India at that age, and, as he says, "It is not so easy to starve at sixty-two as at forty-seven." But now that his work was done, the call home into the presence of the King was a very sudden one, and no one was alarmed about him till a few days before his death. Then he was carried out on an ambulance to Sir Colin Campbell's camp, and a tent pitched for him in a sheltered spot, where the enemy's bullets could no longer threaten the brave warrior or disturb his last moments. Here the dying general was joined by his son Henry, who, with his wounded arm still in a sling, watched at his father's side till the end, and cheered his heart by reading sweet home letters. The doctors could do nothing, and the noble patient himself well knew that the end was near.

But he who could face death at the cannon's mouth could also face it calmly, fearlessly, even gladly, when disease was sent as the messenger to bring him home to his Father's house. "I have so lived for forty years," said he to Outram, "that when death came I might face it without fear." Over and over again he repeated, "I die happy and contented;" then, rejoicing in the hope of eternal life through the merits of the

Saviour he had long faithfully served, he passed peacefully away on the morning of the 24th, bitterly mourned by his brother-generals, and no less so by the few men remaining of the valorous Highlanders he had so often led to the charge.

Under a mango-tree in the gardens of the Alumbagh the hands of his own soldiers tenderly laid the hero to rest, not daring, however, to carve any inscription, for fear the plundering rebel should disturb the sacred spot. A volley was fired over the grave, a rude "H" cut in the bark above it, and then the body of Henry Havelock was sorrowfully left in its lonely resting-place.

But no splendid monument, nor any number of graven words, could ever have honoured the brave soldier so well as did the unbounded admiration and tender regret with which the name of "Havelock" was spoken in every British household when the dread story of Cawnpore and of Lucknow ran from lip to lip throughout the land. Fighting as in his great Captain's sight; faithful to his country because faithful to his God; fearless of the foe because confiding in the care of the divine Friend at his side, Henry Havelock lived to find that fame had come unsought, and that "the path of duty was the way to glory."

THE END.